Dot's school photograph

My Egg-stra Special Family

For my favorite teacher, Dr. Marjorie Hancock. —T. S.

For Matilda, Sarah, and Leon, with love.— D. T.

STERLING CHILDREN'S BOOKS
New York

An Imprint of Sterling Publishing Co., Inc.
1166 Avenue of the Americas
New York, NY 10036

ISBN 978-1-4549-2900-0

Distributed in Canada by Sterling Publishing Co., Inc.
c/o Canadian Manda Group, 664 Annette Street
Toronto, Ontario M6S 2C8, Canada
Distributed in the United Kingdom by GMC Distribution Services
Castle Place, 166 High Street, Lewes, East Sussex BN7 1XU, England
Distributed in Australia by NewSouth Books, University of New South Wales, Sydney, NSW 2053, Australia

For information about custom editions, special sales, and premium and corporate purchases, please contact
Sterling Special Sales at 800-805-5489 or specialsales@sterlingpublishing.com.

Manufactured in China
Lot #:
2 4 6 8 10 9 7 5 3 1
12/18

sterlingpublishing.com

Cover and interior design by Jo Obarowski

A Little Chicken

By Tammi Sauer

Illustrated by Dan Taylor

STERLING CHILDREN'S BOOKS
New York

Dot was a little chicken...

...who, let's face it, was a little chicken.

She was scared of lots of things.

Wolves.

Bears.

The occasional lawn ornament.

Dot tried to be brave, but...

...she just wasn't.

One day, while adding new safety features to the coop,
Dot accidentally bumped a soon-to-be sibling.

The egg rolled out the coop and
down,
down,
down
the hill.

Dot gulped. She knew this wouldn't be over easy.

Then Dot flapped after that egg.

"Aaaaaaaaahhh!"

She just about grabbed it when...

CLUCK-CLUCK.
No luck.

Dot sprang after that egg. "Eeeeeeeeeeeeee!"

She almost had it when...

CLUCK-CLUCK.
No luck.

Dot scrambled after that egg. "Oh! Oh! Oh!"

She was this close when...

snap

The egg bounce-bounce-bounced
into the deep...dark...woods.

Dot's tail feathers shook. But...

This was no time to be a little chicken.

Dot fluttered past one stunned wolf,

two startled bears,

and three very questionable lawn ornaments.

And Dot caught that egg!

* crack-crack-crack *

Dot had a baby sister.

She also had a fan club.

These days, Dot's still scared of lots of things.

But that's okay.

...is just a little chicken.

Dot at three months old

Baby Dot crying at her shadow

Mom, Dad & Dot